Book 2

Twin Soul series

Cloud Conqueror

Winner Twins

And

Todd McCaffrey

Books by The Winner Twins and Todd McCaffrey

Nonfiction:

The Write Path: World Building

Fantasy:

Winter Wyvern

Cloud Conqueror

Books by The Winner Twins

Nonfiction:

The Write Path: Navigating Storytelling

Science Fiction:

The Strand Prophecy

Extinction's Embrace

PCT: Perfect Compatibility Test

Books by Todd McCaffrey

Science fiction

City of Angels

The Jupiter Game

Collections

The One Tree of Luna (And Other Stories)

Dragonriders of Pern® Series

Dragon's Kin

Dragon's Fire

Dragon Harper

Dragonsblood

Dragonheart

Dragongirl

Dragon's Time

Sky Dragons

Non-fiction

Dragonholder: The Life And Times of Anne McCaffrey

Dragonwriter: A tribute to Anne McCaffrey and Pern

Dedication

Dedicated to the marvelous people of
Comic-Con International.

Contents

Chapter One: The Airship Spite

"**S**trangest ship I've ever seen!" someone swore in the crowd nearby. The comment, however rude, was not without merit. The ship had a hull but no rudder, a bowsprit but no masts.

"'Tis not a ship, fool! It's an *air*ship!"

"An airship?"

"It flies in the clouds!"

"There are no masts, only those large balloons!" There were ten large balloons straining at their bonds to the ship, trying to flee into the sky above, arranged into two rows of four with the final two perched atop.

"They lift the ship into the sky!"

"Shh, the Queen approaches!"

Queen Arivik, accompanied by Crown Prince Nestor, walked gingerly down the steps and up the gantry set by the prow of the strange vessel. Both were

dressed in expensive green silk and wore crowns of white coral — rare materials said to be given directly by Ametza, their patron goddess.

Captain Ford, as befit his station, walked three steps behind the last noble, even if it was his ship in the first place.

"You'll be getting the most powerful ship ever!" the first minister, Mannevy, had told him.

"I'll be losing my livelihood," Ford had replied grumpily.

"You'll be a King's man!"

"I already *am* a King's man!" Ford replied. "How many pirates have I brought to his throne, how many ships have I sunk, all under his letter of marque?"

"And that's why the King chose you for this!" Mannevy replied, as he adjusted his monocle.

Ford had known enough not to protest too wildly: money had changed hands: Captain Ford had changed coats — although he much preferred the functional nautical garb to this... this affront to all his senses. Still, he wore the feathered cockade as required, worked his way around managing the long plumage on his blue jacket — and the gold braid on his sleeves was more rank than he'd ever imagined.

His skin told a story of years in the sun. Ford's blonde hair was tucked back in a ponytail, and he wore a gold earring in each ear - payment for the Ferryman. His weathered look contrasted sharply with Mannevy's, whose ebony skin was soft with no wrinkles and whose dark hair was tightly coiled and cut short.

"The first among many, and you'll be the admiral!" the first minister had promised in a rich bass voice. Ford had known the King — and his promises — long enough to know to take *that* with a large grain of salt.

"In the name of my husband, good King

Markel —" the queen's words brought Ford back to the present "— I commission this ship the royal airship *Spite*."

Ford couldn't help smiling to himself: up until a month ago, his ship had been the good ship *Sprite* but in the aftermath of dealing with the Crown Prince, his mother the queen, and the shadow of the man that had once been a proper King, he'd decided in the dead of night to change the name to something more appropriate.

The queen splashed the holy water on the prow and everyone applauded, some only for the joy of the occasion, others because it meant they could go off to their afternoon meal. Crown Prince Nestor, turned his pale face toward Ford, brows furrowed in a demanding look. Ford bit back a harsh retort — the child pretending to be a man! — and turned to the end of the gangway.

And now I command His Majesty's Airship Spite, Ford thought to himself. He surveyed the length of what had once been a very jaunty two-masted brig

 14 Cloud Conqueror

and bit back an oath. The masts were gone. In their place were ten large balloons filled with a magical air that could raise the ship from the ground. At her rear, where the proud rudder had once been mounted was nothing. At the stern, instead, were two large upright spars with large furled vanes of strong cloth.

It looks like a two-tailed peacock, Ford thought ruefully to himself.

"Ship's crew, man your stations!" Ford barked, moving up the walkway to take his place at the helm. A rush of feet followed behind him and took their places, although Ford knew full well that some were already aboard, stoking that never-to-be-sufficiently-damned coal burner set just before the wheel to provide heat and steam for the thaumaturgy that would propel his ship into the sun-drenched sky.

"Stations manned and ready, sir!" Boatswain Knox bellowed from his place by the wheel.

"Prepare to release mooring lines!" Ford called. He turned toward the infernal machine not ten paces in front of him. "Mage, prepare the lifting spells!"

"How many times, Mr. Ford, must I remind you, I'm a thaumaturge —"

"It's Captain Ford and if I call you a mage on my ship, then a *mage* you shall be, sir!" Ford roared back, drowning out the thin young man dressed in purple robes. The mage looked ready to argue so Ford took a step forward and gestured upwards commandingly.

"Aye sir," the mage said in a smaller voice, "at your command."

"Are we ready?" Ford said in a lower voice to the boatswain. Boatswain Knox looked around to all his people and nodded. The boatswain was short and muscular, his fine black hair beginning to thin. Like Ford, Knox's skin was sea-weathered and he wore a gold earring in each ear.

"Wait!" a voice called from the prow by the gantry. "I shall join you on this magnificent journey!"

"Oh, cripes, it's his nibs," Knox muttered.

"That's Prince Nestor, Knox," Ford growled. "Never forget that. If he heard you call him 'his nibs,'

he'd have you flogged.

He turned back to the prince.

"We would be delighted to have you on this most dangerous voyage," Ford called down the length of the ship. "Crewmen, help your prince aboard."

"Look at him, he's turning green already," Knox muttered as the Crown Prince paled at the words: 'most dangerous.'

"If he pukes, you'll be cleaning it up, Knox," Ford warned the man.

"He'll have the best view at the bow, sir," Knox replied, waving forward. "I'll let Doyle know to escort him there."

"You do that," Ford agreed with a half-smile. He scanned the length of his ship and called, "Single up all lines!" He waited while one set of ropes securing the ship to the docks were pulled away. Then he said to the mage, "Prepare to lift ship!" He turned to the mechanic, "Prepare to deploy propellers!"

"Aye, sir!" Mechanic Newman said, saluting

smartly.

"I already said I was —" the mage started irritably.

"Release all lines!" Ford shouted. He turned then to the mage, "Lift ship!"

With a heavy sigh, the purple-robed mage turned toward the bow and raised his arms upwards in the lifting incantation.

"Check all rigging!" Ford shouted to his idlers. He didn't need one of the lifting balloons to come loose.

Slowly, with great reluctance, the good ship *Spite* floated upwards. Ford looked down below him waiting until the keel was clear of the highest spire before turning to the mechanic, "Deploy propellers!"

On either side of the stern the large booms lowered and locked in place. The feather-like cloths unfurled and turned to lock, one at each corner of the compass to form giant four-bladed propellers which began turning, slowly at first, until they provided the airship with a steady forward thrust.

"Adjust for level sailing!" Ford ordered, wondering just *how* his mixed crew would respond. It was the first time he'd issued the order for effect — all other times it had been on a ship that was being fitted out for the King's latest venture.

"Check the rigging!" Knox added to the idlers who scurried about, checking to ensure that all the ropes holding the balloons were taut and none were chafing.

"Oh, my goodness!" a voice wailed from the bow. "We're ever so much higher than I'd imagined!"

"He's fainted!" Doyle called in alarm. "You lot, come help me bring him below!"

"Apparently His Majesty has become a bit overwhelmed with excitement," Ford remarked tartly to the boatswain.

"Indeed, sir!" Knox agreed. "Fortunately, we've lost naught in the change!"

"What heading, sir?" the helmsman asked.

"Take us toward the coast, lad," Ford replied. "I'd like to see how she handles a real wind."

"Aye sir!"

"I'm not sure how the prince will fair it," Knox muttered loudly enough for others nearby to hear and grin.

"It's the way of all landlubbers to wobble a bit when finding their footing on a ship," Ford allowed diplomatically, casting an eye on the mage, Reedis. The other must have sensed his gaze for he turned back and bowed deeply.

"Carry on mage, carry on!" Ford called to him with a half-bow of his own. The mage might be strange and in purple but he clearly knew his stuff.

"Shall I have us go higher?"

"No, I think we should be close to the ground for now," Ford replied. Mage Reedis agreed with a nod.

Chapter Two: The Crown Prince

The shoreline approached at a leisurely pace, so much so that Ford, called to the mechanic, "Can we increase speed?"

The mechanic nodded toward the coal-blacked sailors — no, *airmen*, Ford corrected himself — who grinned in response.

"We're only running at half pressure, sir," Newman assured him. "Shall we go full out?"

"No, save that for later," Ford replied. "Let's try two-thirds power, if you would."

Newman knuckled his forehead in a salute and turned to the stokers. "You heard the captain, lads, let's see some effort!"

"When we get to the new power level, I'll relieve you if you want," Ford said to the stokers. He knew that stoking a steam boiler was hard work and

he prided himself on sparing his men when possible.

In a few minutes the airship noticeably increased speed and the coast rapidly came into view.

A stiff offshore breeze slowed their progress measurably but Ford was still impressed. He glanced to the boatswain who nodded in appreciation.

"We're sailing straight in to the wind," Knox said in awe.

"We're *flying* straight into the wind," Ford corrected him with a twitch of his lips.

"Aye sir, that we are," Knox agreed. "That we are."

"Once we get over the sea, I'll have us reverse course," Ford said. He turned and let his eyes scan the deck from stern to prow. All seemed in order. "Lieutenant Havenam!"

"Sir!" the red-haired first lieutenant jogged from his place amidships back to the helm, saluting his captain properly, his wiry build was well-muscled and topped with a short curled mane of red hair.

"Are you ready to take her over, Sam?" Ford asked.

Havenam's face burst into a huge grin for a brief moment before he schooled his expression into a proper officer's stern gaze. "I believe I am, sir."

Ford grinned back at him. "Good! Then, sir, let's be about it."

"Sir, I relieve you," Havenam said in all seriousness.

"Mr. Havenam, I stand relieved," Ford said. The first lieutenant came to attention and saluted his captain. "Mr. Havenam has the watch!" Captain Ford called through the length of the ship. In a normal voice he said, "I'll be below, Sam, if you need me."

"Aye sir," Havenam replied. "Did I hear correctly that we're to reverse course when we're properly over the sea?"

"You did," Ford agreed. "But I'll amend those orders. Steer out to sea, then back to the Westing lighthouse before you turn back to shore. Go full around the Westing lighthouse — show them what

we can do — and then back home."

Havenam's eyes widened with surprise and delight. "Aye sir. Out to sea, back to the Westing lighthouse, circle it, and then back to the capital."

"You have your orders," Ford said, exchanging salutes before turning to the hatchway. He turned back to call over his shoulder. "And send the watch below."

"Aye sir!" Havenam replied. "All hands, watch below! First watch, man your stations!"

Ford was in his cabin before the second and third watches came scuttling down the hatchway to their quarters.

Ford had just enough time to settle at his desk before someone was pounding on his door.

"Sir, sir! The prince is awake and calling for you!" a sailor — no, *airman* — called nervously.

"Escort him to my quarters, please," Ford

replied. "And ask the cook to provide us with some tea."

"Aye sir," the man replied.

Another knock on his door warned him of the prince's arrival. Ford rose to greet the haggard young man courteously but Prince Nestor was having none of it.

"I shall not have it said that I was inconvenienced on this first voyage, Captain!" Nestor said as soon as the door opened.

"Inconvenienced, your majesty?" Ford replied, his brows creased in question.

"I heard your men snickering!" Nestor said, his voice rising in a whine. "I am the Crown Prince, I will be king someday and all shall fear me."

"As they do now, your highness," Ford agreed. "If you heard the men act inappropriately, I assure you it was not directed at you, sire."

"If not me, then who?" the prince demanded.

"Why seaman — or should I say, *airman* — Lubber, your highness," Ford replied. 'Seaman

Lubber' was the name given to the non-existent worst crewman. Ford was certain that the Prince — no sailor he, let alone *airman* — was not familiar with the name.

"Airman Lubber?"

"Yes, your majesty," Ford replied. He spread his hands expansively. "I'm afraid I made a poor choice in him, your majesty. Only he was an orphan and now he's got a wife and she's expecting so I took pity on him when he applied — even though I'd been warned that he'd heave his guts —" Ford noted with enthusiasm the way the prince turned slightly green at the phrase "— at the first opportunity."

The prince started to reply just as lieutenant Havenam ordered the ship to turn to port and the airship heeled in the wind. "What's that?"

"We're turning, your highness," Ford replied. "I don't doubt that the wind's pushing us over a bit as we're going broadside to it."

The prince stared at him wide-eyed just as someone knocked on the door.

"If you'll be seated, your majesty, I sent for tea," Ford said.

"I'm not thirsty," the prince said, even while taking his chair.

"Would you permit me, I'm rather parched," Ford said. Prince Nestor gave him a jerky nod. Ford waved the crewman inside and nodded politely as the tea was placed on the center depression in the table.

"When you get a moment," Ford said to the crewman, "please inquire after the mage and see if he requires refreshment."

The man gave him a jerky nod in response and Ford thawed enough to add, "He'll probably just want some tea, don't worry."

"Aye sir," the airman returned, knuckling his forehead in acknowledgement.

"Do you think that's wise?" the prince asked as the airman turned away. Ford raised an eyebrow in inquiry. "If Reedis gets distracted won't we all die?"

"Mage Reedis assures me that his magic is

contained, sire," Ford said. "He uses it only when we need to go up or down. Other times he is completely at his leisure."

"That's not what he told *me*," the prince said darkly.

"Perhaps he was unclear," Ford said. "I know that I have seen the effect of the spells on the magic air balloons and how they have maintained their buoyancy without his direct attention."

"If we crash, *captain*, I shall have your head," the prince promised.

Ford managed a small nod, raised the teapot and gestured toward the prince's cup. "Are you sure you won't indulge?"

Prince Nestor shook his head with a shudder.

Captain Ford held back a sigh and raised his cup to his lips partly to refresh himself and partly to hide the fact that he had absolutely nothing to say to the man opposite him.

"When were you planning on drilling the guns, captain?" Nestor asked after the silence grew

oppressive.

"Why, sire, I had thought on our maiden voyage —"

"My father will want to know that his ship is fully capable of dealing with dragons and other aerial menaces, captain," Nestor broke in frostily. "I'm certain that he'd be *very* disappointed if you could not tell them the state of your weaponry upon our return."

"Sire," Ford said slowly, "we still have not planned on how to arrange targets for our guns —"

"Deck there!" a lookout shooted. "Something in the clouds to port!"

Nestor shot to his feet. "There's your target, captain!"

"Indeed, we'll certainly want a look," Ford agreed, placing his cup on the table and rising briskly from his chair.

Chapter Three: The Cannon's Fire

O n deck, Lieutenant Havenam saluted quickly then pointed to the prow. "I have Senten and Marder out on the bowsprit, sir."

"Good," Ford said with a quick nod. "I'll take a look myself."

"Is there anything I can do?" Mage Reedis asked as Ford and the Prince passed him by.

"See if you can bring us to the same altitude," Ford said giving the man an encouraging look.

"Aye, captain!" Reedis replied surprisingly.

"I think I'll rate him mate," Ford said to himself as they continued on their way.

"He should be an officer," said the prince who'd overheard him.

"If I do that it'll go to his head," Ford replied. "No, I think I will warrant him as an airmate, first

class."

The prince scowled at him but said nothing as they neared the bowsprit. The ship's original bowsprit had been maintained even though it no longer had the support of the stay lines rigged from the foremast. And there were no sails hung beneath it. The catwalk had been widened and safety nets strung below in a poor attempt at providing the lookouts with a sense of protection from any mishap that might cause them to slip from their perches.

"Are you coming?" Ford called over his shoulder as he started his way out on the broad spar supported only by his nimble feet.

The prince, eyes wide with fright, shook his head once in a quick jerk and stood, transfixed, as Ford waved a hand and continued running down the bowsprit toward the forward lookouts.

"What have you got?" Ford asked as straddled the bowsprit just behind the two lookouts.

"I saw it first to port, sir," airman Senten said, pointing toward a bank of clouds.

"Then I spotted it — or maybe another — down and starboard, sir," Marder added.

"What does he mean 'starboard'?" the prince called from the safety of the deck.

"Starboard is the side of the ship that's on the right when looking down from the stern toward the bow," Boatswain Knox explained, coming up to the prince's side. "'Port' is on the left as you're looking forward."

"Why not say left and right, then?" the prince asked petulantly.

"Because, sire, left and right depend upon where you're looking," the boatswain said patiently, "while port and starboard always mean the same thing."

"Another?" Captain Ford asked the lookouts, shaking his head in dismay at the prince's ignorance.

"It was smaller, golden, and very fast," Marder said. "Wasn't the same as the first one?"

"And the other?"

"It was a dragon, sir," Senten said, "I'd stake my life on it."

"Let's hope you won't have to," Ford said. He turned around, hopped back up on top of the bowsprit and raced his way back to the deck, calling, "All hands, man the guns!" He lifted his cockade hat and waved high above his head in signal to Havenam at the far end of the ship, shouting, "Battle stations!"

"Battle stations, aye sir!" Havenam shouted back to him. He turned to the ship's boy and shouted, "Beat to quarters!"

The little boy grabbed his drum and started rattling on it with his drumsticks. From below airmen boiled up, racing toward the guns and the gun tackle. Powder and shot were brought up and slow matches lit from the boiler's fire. The entire ship's crew, thirty-six strong, were now on deck or at their stations.

Spite was a small ship. She carried only eight

six-pound cannon, four on each side. Each cannon took a crew of four — so the ship could only man one side of guns and still sail.

On the sea, Ford had never needed more than that because his brig had been quick on the stays — she'd turn around in less than a ship's length — and he'd trained his crew to perfection. Up here in the air, he wondered if he should split his crew to allow him to have guns manned on both sides. He was about to order it when he looked to starboard and realized that his home town was sprawled below him. Any shot to the right of the ship would land on the town.

He crossed to the port side of the ship and nodded as second lieutenant Jens touched his hat and reported, "All guns manned and ready, sir."

"Very good," Ford said, returning the salute. "Be on the lookout, and be ready to fire on my command."

"Aye sir."

And then they waited. Ford returned to the bow to question the two lookouts.

"What color and size were they?" Ford asked them. "And about how far off would you say?"

"I'm new at guessing distances up here in the air, sir," Marder replied slowly, "but if they were on the sea, I'd say they were within a league of us, maybe less."

"One seemed gold with bits of red — that was the smaller one, sir," Senten reported. "It seemed a fair bit faster, too." He frowned before adding, "It seemed to me like they were cavorting, sir."

"Cavorting?"

"Playing, sir," Marder added in support of his fellow lookout. "And the big one was black with bits of red — near about half the size of the ship, certainly the size of a good house."

"So not the size of a brig," Ford replied. "But half." He could see the two men relaxing as the difference in size relieved their worries. He smiled at them, "Nothing we haven't beaten before, then."

"No, sir," Marder agreed. "At least, as a ship on the sea."

Ford waved a hand at the air and clouds around them. "This is our new sea now, lads."

"Aye sir," Senten said in a wary tone.

"Keep a good lookout," Ford said, turning back to the stern of the ship. "I think we'll see if our cavorters can be encouraged to visit us."

"Sir?" Marder asked.

"It's time to drill the guns, I think," Ford said. He raised his voice to carry the length of the ship as he called, "All hands, prepare to fire guns!"

Lieutenant Jens ran over to meet him. "What target, sir?"

Ford came to the port side and looked about. Finally he pointed to a cloud in the distance. "Aim for that," he said, "let's see what we can smoke out."

Enlightenment dawned on the young man's face. "You're hoping to attract them to us, then, sir?"

"Indeed," Ford said. He waved to the gun crews. "We're going to see what a broadside in the air sounds like, men."

The crew gave a cheer but it was half-hearted.

"What about the dragons?" the prince called. "What are you going to do about them?"

"I'm hoping to get their attention, sire," Ford told him with as much calm as he could muster. *Really!*

The prince thought about it and nodded. To the gun crews he shouted, "You men! A guinea to the first crew who hits the dragon!"

That brought a much louder cheer from the crews.

"Fire in succession," Ford said, turning to lieutenant Jens who nodded.

"Gun number one, set bearing," Jens said, walking back to the aftermost gun. "Ready, fire!"

The gun captain lit the fuze and stood back just as the little six-pounder roared and reared back against its moorings. Black smoke billowed from its muzzle and captain Ford drew his telescope to train it on the flying ball in the distance.

"Stop your vents!" the gun captain roared to his crew. "Swab her out!" an airman rammed a wet

swab down the barrel. "Charge the weapon!" A bag of powder was placed into the barrel followed by a wad of cloth. "Ram home!" The swabber rammed the cartridge down. The gun captain went to the touch hole with his long pricker and pricked open the powder bag. "Home!" he called, followed by, "Load shot!" The six-pound shot and another wad of cloth were loaded in. "Ram home!" A moment later, he shouted, "Run out!"

The men strained on the tackles to pull the gun back to firing position. Satisfied, the gun captain turned and saluting lieutenant Jens, said, "Gun number one ready to fire, sir!"

"Very good, Marsters," Jens said. He turned to the second gun. "Gun number two, prepare to fire!"

"Captain!" Senten called from the bow. "I see them!"

"Hold your fire!" Ford shouted to the gun crew. "Senten, where away?"

"Fine off the starboard bow, sir!"

Ford turned to the indicated direction, squinted,

and then nodded. He turned back to Jens. "Fire the second gun."

"Sir?" Jens asked.

"What are you doing?" the prince shouted. "The dragon is over there, shoot it!"

"So is our town, sire," Ford replied with all the calm he could muster. "Our shots will fall down regardless of what they hit first." The prince looked at him in confusion. "Do you believe the king will thank us if we shell his town?"

"So why fire, then?" the prince demanded.

"I intend to give them a good target," Ford replied. The prince's brow rose in consternation, so Ford pointed his finger to the deck, saying, "Us." He turned back to Jens. "Fire number two."

"Aye, sir!" Jens called, knocking off a quick salute. "Gun number two, fire when ready!"

"Aye sir!" A short time later the second gun barked, hurling itself inwards and its shell out toward the distant cloud and the fields below.

Ford frowned and gestured for the first

lieutenant. Lieutenant Havenam came at a trot and saluted, even as his sides heaved from his exertion.

"I regret our lack of masts," Ford said to him. Havenam gave him a surprised look. "I wish we could get a look from higher up."

"Two thoughts, sir," Havenam replied after a moment. Ford gestured for him to say more. "I could climb to the top of the highest balloon. That would give us a better range." Ford nodded and gestured for him to continue. "Later, if we have time, we could perhaps rig an independent balloon to carry a man aloft."

"Good suggestions, both," Ford agreed, clapping his lieutenant on the shoulder. "Let's do the first now, and talk with our mage about the second at a later date."

"Aye, sir," Havenam said, grinning. He started toward the ratlines that girded the sides of the ship and attached her to the balloons raising them into the air. As he started to climb, he called back to his captain, "I've been itching to do this for quite some

time!"

"Well, enjoy it then," Ford called back. "As soon as you demonstrate the joys of riding on the tops of balloons, I've no doubt that we'll have more than enough volunteers to replace you!"

Havenam grinned again and scrambled up and over the top of the nearest balloon.

"And Sam?" Ford called after him. The first lieutenant looked down at him. "Don't fall, it's bad form!"

"Aye, sir!" Sam Havenam agreed with a laugh. A moment later he was out of sight, obscured by the balloons.

Ford sought out Reedis. "That will work, won't it? Having one of our men at the tops of your balloons?"

"It should be safe enough, provided they don't puncture them," Reedis allowed. He made a face, then added, "Although it might be wise to bring up a spare from the holds just in case."

"And how soon can you make it ready when

we bring it up?"

Reedis pulled on his chin in thought. "Five, maybe ten minutes," he allowed. He waved at the ballon above them. "Mind you, it'll take a lot out of me. I won't be good for more magic for another fifteen minutes or so, after."

"Even with the help of the gods?"

"That's counting on their help," Reedis replied. "And their good will, too."

"Then we shall do all in our power to retain their goodwill," Ford promised, clapping the man on the shoulder. Reedis looked at his shoulder where Ford had touched it with an odd expression. For a moment, Ford wondered whether the mage would take offense but then the man grinned up at him.

"If I may, sir," Reedis said, emboldened, "it might not be best to offend Ophidian, given that we are here in the sky."

"Ah, but we're over Ametza's realm and our ship is powered by steam," Ford countered. "And you know how Ametza feels about other gods."

"I do," Reedis replied. "Still, we might do our best to avoid Ophidian's wrath."

"The King has commissioned us to keep the wyverns and dragons from raiding his lands, mage," Ford told him sternly. "In that, we will not fail."

"Deck there!" Lieutenant Havenam shouted from above. "I see them! They're coming this way!"

"Jens, fire gun number three!" Ford commanded, turning away from the mage and back to the business at hand.

The third gun barked and its smoke blew back across the deck. Ford turned to the mechanic, "Mr. Newman, how quickly can we get more speed?"

"It'd be best if you relieved the stokers, sir," Newman replied. "After that, five minutes and we can be at full power."

"Very well, make it so," Ford said.

"Do you think that wise, captain?" the prince asked.

Ford shrugged. "We've got to know our best speed sometime, sire. And with luck, we'll be faster

than the beasts we're chasing."

The prince thought on that for a moment and nodded. "One thing, captain."

"Sire?"

"When it comes to shooting at the beasts, I shall be the gunner," the prince said.

"Sire," Ford spluttered, "with all reverence, you've not the experience!"

"And this is how I'll get it," the prince said. "When we kill the beast, the blow shall be mine."

Nestor the Dragonkiller, Ford thought to himself, *with that title he'll have no trouble taking the kingdom.* Ford wasn't so sure that he liked the idea of Nestor as king.

"We may not be able to time the shot, sire," Ford temporized.

"It shall be *my* shot, sir, depend upon it!"

"On deck! The beasties have come around and they're heading our way!"

"Let's give them something more to consider," Ford said. He shouted back to the boatswain, "Bring

us ten degrees to starboard." To lieutenant Jens he said, "Fire number four when we're on the new course."

"Aye, sir!"

Ford grabbed his telescope and moved starboard to peer over the side in the direction Lieutenant Havenam had indicated. He looked and scanned and then — "I have them!"

Bang! Gun number four blasted the air to port.

"Jens!" Ford shouted. The lieutenant turned toward him. "I want a skew elevation — gun one down, gun two steady, and gun three pointed up — and be prepared to broadside on my command."

"Aye, sir!" Jens replied, bellowing orders to the three guns that were ready while the crew of the fourth hastened to reload their weapon.

"Mr. Reedis!" Ford called, promoting the mage with his words. The mage looked toward him from where he was supervising the unfurling of a spare balloon. "How quickly can you lower us?"

"Sir?" Reedis said, confused.

"The beasties are about to cross under our hull," Ford explained. "I want to let them and drop to their level where I'll fire a broadside."

"How far below us?"

"Not more than a hundred feet, I'd say," Ford said, peering through the lens of his telescope to confirm his estimate.

"I can get us down a hundred feet in less than a minute," Reedis allowed.

"And can you do more, after?"

"I'll be a bit drained for probably the next several minutes," Reedis admitted. "The spells take energy and thought."

"Very well, be prepared on my command," Ford said.

"Aye, sir," Reedis replied. Ford began to think that he might actually come to like the purple mage. Always, leadership was about learning how to inspire, he reminded himself.

"They're closing," Ford now called, his voice in unison with Lieutenant Havenam from the balloons

above. "Steady, steady... Now! Reedis, lower us! Jens, fire when sighted!"

Spite practically fell from the sky. For a moment captain Ford feared that the mage had lost his abilities and they were going to plummet to their deaths. But the ship seemed to find its footing, even as several airmen lost theirs at the sudden maneuver. From above, Havenam let out a surprised cry and Ford looked up to see his first lieutenant flailing above, reaching for a handhold before climbing back up, clearly unprepared for the fall.

"Targets in sight!" Jens called. "Steady, steady... fire!"

The three guns roared out and pushed *Spite* sideways in the air with their recoil even as Jens' gun captains bellowed, "Stop your vents!"

"Number four gun, ready, sir!" the gun captain of the fourth gun shouted.

"Fire as you bear!" Ford called back, turning to watch the shot and the dragons — no, the white one was smaller and hand only two legs, not four...

a wyvern, then.

"We're going to hit the black one!" someone cried.

The prince ran forward. "No! No, that's *my* shot!"

Ford ran to the port side, following the one ball that had been aimed level as it tore through the air straight toward the large black dragon.

But the smaller gold wyvern turned in the air and practically jumped up in the path of the ball — *crack!* — even from the hundreds of yards distance, Ford could hear the bones on the wyvern shatter. The wyvern pierced the air with a dying cry and crumpled, falling like nothing more than an old sack of cloth toward the ground.

The black dragon roared with anger, first diving toward the stricken wyvern and then, in an instant, turning back to roar at the *Spite.*

And that was when it opened its jaws and let out a burst of flame.

"Reedis, drop the ship!" Ford ordered as the

dragon rose to their level, its jaws opened to spew another gout of flame in their direction. "Idlers, man the buckets! We've got to wet her down!'

The four idlers, who'd been pressed into helping with the gun crews, grabbed their buckets and started dousing the sides of the ship to give it what little protection against flame that they could.

At the same time, Reedis closed his eyes and waved his arms — and *Spite* fell from the sky.

"Steer towards the water!" Ford shouted to the helmsman. "We stand a chance if we can make the harbor!"

The sudden drop had surprised the dragon who seemed to pause in mid-air before diving down to the tops of the balloons, roaring in fury. A desperate shout matched it and Ford turned to see Lieutenant Havenam falling from the balloons above.

"Sam!" Ford cried as his long-time friend fell toward the side of the ship. He had just a moment to meet his friend's eyes before Havenam bounced sickeningly off the side rail and fell toward the ground

below. In the distance, Ford saw a field of blue, and a house and large barn not too far from it. The white of the wyvern's crumpled form was visible against the blue of the flowers in the field. *Wyvern flowers.*

"Gunners, another broadside for that bastard!" Ford shouted.

"I shall take a gun!" the prince cried, running to push lieutenant Jens aside and taking a place at gun number two.

Spite was still falling.

"Newman!" Ford shouted. "Full speed!"

Spite had turned and was bearing toward the coastline even as she fell from the sky.

"Mr. Reedis!" Ford shouted. "We can't hit the ground!"

"Aye, sir," Reedis said, his whole body trembling. "I'll do my best."

"If you don't, we'll all die," Ford warned him.

A ghost of a smile crossed the weedy mage's lips before he answered, "Then I'll do my best, sir."

"Cook!" Ford called. "A tot of rum for the air

mage!"

A head popped up from the hatchway, eyes wide with fright and surprise.

"I don't think he drinks, sir," the cook allowed.

"Then some tea, and be quick about it," Ford said. "And get a tot of rum for all the stokers."

A cheer went up from the coal-blackened men surrounding the boiler that seemed to glow bright red above the steel plate that protected the ship from its fiery contents.

"Mr. Newman," Ford called, "we've got to make the harbor before we hit the ground."

"The lads are stoking flat out, sir," Newman replied. "This is as fast as we go."

Ford turned to look for the dragon but it had disappeared from his sight. "Marder! Senten! Where away the dragon?"

A moment later the two lookouts called back, "No sign of it, sir! It disappeared over the town!"

"If it sets the town alight, captain," the prince growled, "you'll pay for it with your head."

Ford thought for a moment. "If we turn, we can give chase but we'll be firing our guns over the town, sire. We may end up doing more damage than good."

The prince glowered at him. "If we get beneath it, we can fire up."

"The balls, even if they hit him, will still fall to the ground, sire," Ford replied slowly, using the same tone he'd use with a foolish child.

The prince turned red. "Needless to say, I wish us to land at our proper dock," the prince said. "Our mother will be waiting for us and there are laurels well won." He paused for a moment. "I killed a wyvern, as all will attest!"

"Begging pardon, sire," said the captain of the number two gun, "but what about our guinea?"

The prince took two quick steps toward the man and slapped him hard on the face. "There is no guinea! It was *I* who took the shot, —" and he hit the helpless airman again "— *I* who killed the creature —" another slap "— and *I* who will wear the laurels!"

He turned to Ford and shouted, "Really, captain, what sort of a crew do you keep?"

Ford locked his jaws and turned his head away to avoid replying to the tyrant in front of him.

Nestor turned from him to shout at Reedis, "We're landing at our dock!"

"Ease off on the boiler," Ford said to Newman. "Helmsman, come about and head us to the docks."

"Aye, sir," the helmsman said, turning the wheel that caused the port side propeller to stop turning while feeding more power to the starboard propeller, causing the ship to turn to port in a leisurely manner. "Bow! Report when you have our dock in sight and lined up!"

"Aye!" came the cry back from Marder. "Dock in sight. Another twenty degrees and we'll be straight on."

Ford took a look around the deck and gestured for Jens to join him. When the lieutenant was within earshot he said, "Secure the guns, dowse the matches, and prepare for docking."

"Aye, sir," Jens said.

"I'm going below," Ford told him. "You have the ship."

"Aye, sir, I have the ship," Jens said loudly.

Without another word, Ford turned to the hatchway and climbed out of the sunlight and into the cool darkness below.

Chapter Four: A Bitter Triumph

Twenty minutes later, he was called back to the deck. In the intervening time, Ford had sat at his chair, writing what he could in his log, and trying to forget the dying scream of Sam Havenam as he fell to his death.

"Ah, you're back," the prince said when he spotted Ford rising to the deck. "We've managed quite well without you."

"I'm glad, sire," Ford replied, ignoring the jab.

"I've had some time to consider our next actions," the prince said even as the ship lowered toward the dock below.

Ford waved a hand palm up, before turning to the mechanic. "Mr. Newman, prepare to feather the propellers on my mark."

"Aye sir, on your mark," Newman agreed.

Ford looked beyond him to the mage. "Mr.

Reedis, how are you?"

"I'm well enough, captain," the purple-robed mage allowed. "Could do with a rest, truth be told."

"Doubtless you'll get it and much rewards from the King," Ford assured him. He glanced forward and toward the ground below. "Is our descent steady now?"

"Aye, sir," Reedis replied. "We're going down at about —"

"Twenty feet a minute, by my guess," Ford interjected.

"Aye, sir," Reedis agreed.

"Good," Ford said. Raising his voice, he called, "Mr. Newman, feather the propellers and prepare to stow them!"

"Aye, sir!" Newman called back.

"You know, sire, no one has ever docked an airship before," Ford remarked calmly to the prince who was pacing nearby.

"I'm sure you'll do well at it," the prince allowed. "When we get docked, I'll want you take a

party —"

"A party, sire?" Ford repeated, brows drawn in a frown. He'd planned on securing the ship, making sure that the balloons were safe and not punctured, emptying the boiler, clearing the ash from the firegrill, and ordering more coal to be brought aboard.

"You know where that beast fell," the prince said. "I want you to find it and bring it back so that I can show everyone what I've done."

"Sire?" was all that Ford could say.

"Get the beast, bring it to the castle, and we'll have a triumph," the prince said tartly. "Then everyone will be able to *see* what I've done."

"Surely, your word is enough —"

"And then I'll have it gutted and stuffed," the prince continued, ignoring Ford's words. "Perhaps we can eat the meat, mother and I. I'm sure dragon meat conveys strength and health."

"It was the wyvern we hit, sire," Ford reminded him gently. He'd had enough time to reflect that the only way to treat this prince — his future king — was

very carefully.

"*I* know what *I* hit, captain!" the prince growled. "And it's your job to make sure that everyone on this ship, everyone in this kingdom, knows it as well!"

"As you say, your highness," Ford replied. He glanced toward the ground below and said, "If you'll excuse me, we're about to land."

"Have our pennants raised, break out the victory signal," the prince commanded.

"We've no masts, sire," Ford protested, "so we packed no pennants."

"An oversight you'll correct as soon as we make landfall, captain," the prince said.

"I could have our ship's boy man the drums," Ford suggested, "that'd get everyone's attention. But I don't doubt that reports of our encounter have preceded us."

"Hmmph," the prince allowed. "I suppose you're right. But *do* get your boy drumming just in case."

Ford gestured for the ship's boy who ran off

to grab his drum and, as the drummer beat a steady tattoo, the crew lined the railings to drop lines to hands waiting below and the ship was pulled down into its dock.

The gantry was raised up from the ground and secured.

"Sire, yours is the honor," Ford said, gesturing to the gantry amidships. The prince nodded in acceptance of his due and made for the planks that led to the ground beside them.

"Behold! I return in triumph!" Prince Nestor shouted from the top of the walkway. His white pasty skin was now red from the sun and covered in soot, his brown hair was wind-blown, disheveled and frizzy.

"I, Nestor, Crown Prince, have slain the wyvern! I have frightened the dragon away from us! Never again shall our kingdom have to fear the air over our heads!"

Queen Arivik rushed up the gantry and grabbed the prince in her arms, crushing him against

her. Her cadaverous body was all bones and angles as she pressed her son tightly against her, her brown hair entangling with his like the serpents of a medusa spiralling down from her coral crown.

"Oh, my son, my son!" she cried. She glared at Ford. "How could you let him get into such danger?"

"I followed the prince's orders, your Majesty," Ford said.

"I must go tell father," Prince Nestor said, pulling his head back from his mother.

"He shall order a triumph!" the queen agreed, turning to head back down the gantry, the prince's hand clasped tightly in hers. "He'll have no reason to doubt you now, my son."

Nestor reddened and turned his head to catch Ford's eyes. "You have your orders, captain."

"As you wish, your highness," Ford said with a deep bow. He waited until the prince turned away again before rising upright. At which point, he called to the crew, "Three cheers for the Prince!"

The crew cheered half-heartedly.

The prince and his mother mounted the royal carriage and were whisked away in the direction of the castle.

"Jens, I'll need a horse immediately and a wagon to follow," Ford said. "Secure the ship, see to the men and then find me."

"Aye sir," Jens said, saluting sharply. "And Mrs. Havenam, sir?"

Ford sighed. "I'll tell her when I can," he said. "He'd want me to tell her personally."

"Aye sir," Jens said in a tone which did not hide his relief at avoiding the odious task.

"Mage Reedis?"

"Captain?"

"Are you up for a ride?" Ford asked the purple-robed mage. Reedis swayed on his feet and shook his head. "Hmm," Ford continued, "perhaps you'd best make use of the bunk in my cabin and get some rest."

"If it's not too much trouble, captain," Reedis agreed, tottering toward the hatchway.

"Mr. Newman," Ford said, looking for coal-

grimed mechanic. Newman bobbed up beside him. "Will you see to your gear, douse the fires, clear the ash, and get more coal aboard?" Newman looked at him in confusion. "I can't say when we'll next need to fly, so I'd like us to be ready."

"Of course, captain," Newman agreed. "After, can I let the men take leave?"

"Of course," Ford agreed. "I would be surprised if we're called to action again this day."

"I'm glad to hear that, captain," Newman replied.

"I'll leave you to it, then," Ford said, moving toward the plank gantry and to the ground below. He could see a seaman leading a pair of horses. He turned back and shouted, "Mr. Knox?"

"Sir?"

"What would you say to a ride in the country?"

"If it's to see where that devil fell, I'd relish it, sir," the boatswain returned, moving to follow his captain off the ship. He glanced over his shoulder. "My mate can manage here."

"Aye, no problem," the boatswain's mate, Needles, called back, easily. "And then I'll join the others ashore."

Ford waved his assent to that and jerked his head to Knox, to hurry him up to the horses.

They mounted and found the easiest way out of the cobblestoned streets and into the roads outside the city proper.

"Did you get a good bearing on where the beastie fell, sir?" Knox asked as they eased their mounts into a slow trot.

Ford nodded and held up a hand, pointing. "That way."

"And Mr. Havenam, sir?"

"Also that way," Ford replied. "That's part of the reason for the wagon."

They rode for a while in silence before Knox said, "Did you understand what her majesty said, about the king and her son, sir?"

Ford grimaced. "I've heard a rumor or two." He glanced at the older man. "And you?"

"There's many a tale told about the queen," Knox allowed. "And not so many about the king before he married her."

Ford's lips twisted upwards. "I'd heard something like that myself."

"There's some that say that the prince is not the king's natural son."

"He's the prince, Knox, and it will never do to forget that," Ford said reprovingly.

"Aye, sir," Knox agreed in a low voice. "I won't."

They rode for many minutes in silence. Captain Ford spent the time thinking. He was the first airship captain, he doubted he'd be the last. When he'd sailed on the sea with a letter of marque from the King he'd made a good living, taking the ships of warring nations and selling them and their cargo at good prices. He'd made a name for himself: a fair rise for an orphan child whose first memories were of the hard life at sea. What sort of money would he get ridding the skies of dragons? Particularly if the

Prince would claim them as his own?

And what would have happened if the dragon had managed to flame their ship? There was no convenient, if raging, sea in which to fall — merely thousands and thousands of feet of thin air. Havenam's death made it clear that falling from an airship was fatal.

Ford felt trapped. He couldn't just give up his ship: he was tied to it. Without it, he was merely a penniless seaman with a few good tales to tell. He'd hitched his fortunes to king and kingdom, he would pay the price or fail utterly.

Which meant, Ford's mind reasoned on, that he would have to find a way to work with the prince — who would one day be King — and work well enough that he kept his head on his shoulders and food in his belly. More than that would be asking too much, he feared.

A whistle in the distance startled him out of his reverie and he looked up to see a train passing by them on the way out to the outlying villages. He

waved at the fireman and the passengers who looked out at them. And then the train turned northwards while he continued toward the west.

They crested a hill and saw a farm not too far in the distance and several fields.

"There," he said, pointing toward a valley full of blue flowers. "That's where it fell."

Knox grunted in acknowledgement and the two of them turned their horses toward the valley.

It was a large valley and the flowers were tall. Ford had expected to see the gold of the wyvern easily and was surprised when he didn't. He and Knox rode all around the valley, scouring it for any sign of the dead beast. Captain Ford was just beginning to wonder whether the beast had been as injured as they'd assumed — perhaps it had slunk off to some lair and was licking its wounds — and wouldn't *that* be the sort of news he'd hate to deliver to the Prince — when Knox called from uphill and waved him over.

"What is it?" Ford asked when he neared

enough for his voice to travel the distance to the other's ears.

"There," Knox said, pointing toward a mound of newly-turned earth.

Captain Ford peered down from his mount at the mound. He frowned and jumped down from his horse to examine the ground close up. "It's too small for something that big."

"Maybe," Knox allowed. He glanced around the far end of the field and pointed. "There's the wagon, maybe they've got a shovel." He pointed to another spot. "And look here, sir! There's crushed flowers like something large fell and there's a path from it to this mound."

"You think to dig it up?" Ford asked. "It looks like a grave, fresh dug."

"Dug today, I'm sure," Knox agreed. "If it's not the wyvern, whoever dug this would know where to find it, wouldn't they?"

Ford thought about it and nodded. He pointed to the large depression with its crushed flowers and

said, "That looks about where the wyvern fell." With a frown, he added, "But I didn't see it land. I was too busy watching Havenam's plunge."

"And the best way to find out who dug this is to find out who's in the dirt," Knox said.

"You're a ghoul, boatswain," Ford grumbled. With a deep sigh, he added, "But I suppose we've little choice, the prince is expecting a triumph."

They shouted for the wagon and saw that it was manned by Marder, the lookout.

"Came as soon as I could, Captain," Marder said as he pulled the wagon to a halt.

"Have you got a shovel with you?" Ford asked.

"I do," Marder replied. "I figured we'd want to do the honors for the lieutenant." He pointed at the mound. "Is that him? Did you find him already?"

"It could be," Ford allowed with a shudder. "But we found this mound, we don't know what's in it."

"A body, I imagine," Knox said. He gestured to Marder. "Throw us that shovel and we'll see."

It took them twenty minutes to dig down to the corpse. It was a woman. She was naked except for a cloth someone had laid over her.

"We should cover her back up," Marder said after a moment. "It's not the lieutenant and it isn't a flying beast, either."

"But look at her," Knox urged. "See how she lies." He pointed toward her leg. "Her leg's been shattered and she was bleeding when she was put here."

"Over here!" Marder called to the others. "There are tracks here," he said, peering down and pointing toward a line of footprints. "A girl's."

"And a man's here," Ford said.

"They weren't together," Knox said. "The grass is recovering from the girl's tracks, she was here just over an hour ago, I'd say."

"Just when we were fighting the wyvern," Ford noted. He pointed toward the grave. "So who is this person?"

"Magic got us in the air, sir," Knox said.

"Perhaps magic is at work here, too?"

"If you look at her legs, she's injured just about the way the wyvern was," Marder said.

"So you're saying this woman was the *wyvern?*" Captain Ford said.

"Maybe," Knox said. "It would explain the tracks. The body was dragged from that great depression — where the wyvern might have landed — to this spot where the woman was buried.

"The Prince is not going to accept a corpse for his triumph," Ford said sourly.

"Perhaps we should look for poor Lieutenant Havenam?" Marder suggested.

"There's a farm nearby, we should go there first," Captain Ford said.

Chapter Five: The Young Apprentice

They were met by a surly young man who insisted that he hadn't heard a thing.

"I was in town," he said. "I'm the apprentice here and my master is resting now. He won't wish to be disturbed."

"Did he see anything?" Captain Ford asked.

"No," the lad said, shaking his head firmly. "He was with me."

"Was there anyone else who stayed here?" Ford asked.

The lad's eyes widened fractionally but he shook his head in vigorous denial. "No one saw anything."

"We found a body," Ford persisted. "A woman's body. She was recently buried."

"That can't be anyone from around here," the lad declared. "I've heard of no one sick in these parts

for the past sennight."

"Very well," Captain Ford said. "We thank you for your time in the name of the Prince."

The lad's eyes flared quickly. "You work for the Prince?"

"I'm the captain of the royal airship," Captain Ford replied. "This is my boatswain, Knox."

The lad gave Knox a quick look and nodded at Ford. "I think I saw your ship flying, earlier."

"Indeed," Captain Ford said. "We fought a dragon and a wyvern."

"We hit the wyvern," Knox added. "We thought it had fallen near here."

"And we lost a man," Ford said, "one of my lieutenants. We're looking for his body."

"That's why we dug up the grave," Knox said, feeling the need for an explanation.

"Oh," the lad said.

"If we need to talk with you again, who should we ask for?" Captain Ford said.

"Angus," the lad replied. "My name is Angus

Franck."

"And your master?" Knox asked with a nod toward his captain. "What is his name?"

Angus gave him a sour look. "He's not to be disturbed, he's old and the day took too much out of him."

"Give us his name," Ford ordered.

"Zebala," Angus said in a surly tone. "Rabel Zebala. He's a smith. I'm his apprentice."

"He works with Ibb, the mechanical, does he not?" Ford asked.

Angus gave a jerky nod in response.

"I know Ibb," Ford said, his tone half-warning.

"We saw him earlier," Angus said. "Now, if you'll excuse me, I've got chores."

"Of course," Ford said, turning away from the door. "Thank you for your time."

Angus watched as they walked away and then, when they turned back toward him, hastily shut the upper and lower halves of the split kitchen door.

Ford gestured for Knox to head toward the

horses. They mounted and rode down the path back toward the main road. A short while later they pulled up their horses beside an abandoned cart.

Marder sprang up from a clump of underbrush and waved at them.

"What did you learn?" Captain Ford asked the man as they pulled up to a halt.

"There were two sets of tracks led to that farm," Marder said. "And there's a forge in the barn —"

"The man's a smith, works with Ibb," Ford said.

" — crazy ol' clanker," Marder muttered.

"Captain likes him," Knox warned.

"What else?" Ford prompted, motioning for Knox to leave off.

"I found a shovel, it was dirty, like it had been used to dig sometime today," Marder said.

"Did only one set of tracks come back?" Knox asked. He glanced at the captain. "Perhaps they buried the girl we found."

"Then why deny it?" Ford asked. The other two shook their heads in puzzlement.

"The tracks of the man, the one that came back, they were heavier than the ones on the way to the field," Marder said with a sour look. His jaundiced skin and bulging eyes making him look nearly a corpse himself. He wore only silver earrings in both ears.

"He was carrying something?" Captain Ford wondered.

"Or someone," Knox suggested.

"None of this gets us nearer to our missing wyvern," Ford said.

"It seems like the King ought to look into this," Marder suggested. The other two looked at him like he was crazy. "Well, aren't we supposed to get the King's justice?" He pointed back toward the field of blue flowers. "And doesn't that poor soul deserve some of it?"

"Are you saying she was murdered?"

"She's dead," Marder replied. "That's all I'm saying." He chewed his lip for a moment before

adding, "And she was injured just like she took our cannonball."

"We should look for Lieutenant Havenam's body," Captain Ford said after a moment's thoughtful silence. "Maybe we'll find the wyvern, too."

"He might be only the next field over," Marder said hopefully. Captain Ford nodded and turned back to mount his horse.

"Follow us," Ford ordered Marder as he and Knox set their horses off to a slow walk.

They found Lieutenant Havenam's body two fields over, in a small forest of trees.

"It looks like he landed in the trees, then fell through them to the ground below," Marder said as they bent over the ruined remains of the handsome officer.

"Mmm," Captain Ford agreed, moving further into the trees and hoisting himself up. He climbed swiftly and found himself out of the foliage with a good view of the land around.

"What do you see, Captain?" Knox shouted up from

the ground below.

"I've got a bit of cloth, sir, I can cover Mr. Havenam up and put him in the wagon, if you'd like," Marder added.

"Do that," Ford said. "Mr. Knox, please join me."

"I'll help Marder first, if that's okay," the boatswain replied.

"Of course," the captain said. "Marder, if you're in for a climb after all your exertions, you are welcome to join us."

Marder made a noncommittal noise. From below, Captain Ford could hear the two men lifting the body into the wagon and the sound of harsh fabric being drawn over. He hadn't the heart to do it himself — or rather, his heart would burst if he had to cover his friend's ignominiously destroyed body. He and Havenam had been midshipmen together on old Seneer's *Retribution*: they were close. So he kept his gaze off to the distance where the scarring of the field beyond showed the destruction of the wyvern's flowers as a patch of brown in a field of blue. And beyond it he could see trampled flowers leading toward the dark brown of the grave they'd found.

A sound from below alerted him to the ascent of his

two crewmen. A moment later, their heads appeared beside him and he gestured silently into the distance. Knox and Marder followed his hand and gazed at the same torn ground he'd been watching while they were busy with the body.

"Whatever fell there was dragged to the grave and buried there," Marder said.

"Aye, I'd say the same," Knox agreed.

"So what do we tell the prince?" Captain Ford said. "He's expecting a wyvern's body and a triumph."

The other two shook their heads in silence.

"Mrs. Havenam, should see her first?" Knox asked, dodging the question.

Captain Ford jerked a nod. By unspoken agreement they started back down the tree and to the wagon waiting below.

"We should go then, shouldn't we?" Marder asked, gesturing toward the town. "It'll be full dark when we return."

"Aye," Ford agreed.

Chapter Six: A Wyvern's Corpse

"I promised my father a wyvern's corpse, Mr. Ford!" Crown Prince Nestor roared when Ford met him hours later. "How am I to receive a reward, if I can't show the body?"

"It's Captain Ford, Sire," Ford said. "We looked for the body and found nothing."

"Except maybe that strange woman," Knox put in feebly. The boatswain had offered to accompany the captain after they'd paid their respects to Mrs. Havenam.

"I have heard enough about that nonsense!" Nestor snapped. "How can you expect my father to believe that the woman was the wyvern?"

"Sire, I know very little of magic and I haven't had a chance to talk to Mage Reedis," Ford replied. "Perhaps one of the court magicians would know

something more?"

"If you'd wanted their opinion, why didn't you bring them the body?" the prince demanded.

"We thought it might not be a good idea to bring a woman's corpse to the royal palace, Sire," Ford said.

The prince bit back a violent retort as the image formed in his imagination. "No," he agreed, "that might not be the best of ideas."

"We can bring one of your mages back to the site," the boatswain offered.

"First, perhaps, we could just ask?" Ford suggested.

"Not possible," the prince said, shaking his head violently.

Ford's brow creased in question.

"They are a bunch of tattering old women," the prince explained. "If I ask them, you can be certain my father — and the whole kingdom — will know of it in no time."

"And…" Ford said, reflecting his confusion.

"Could you imagine how it would get out?" Nestor demanded. He changed his voice to something that sounded remarkably like his royal father. "'The prince killed a woman and wants to say she was a monster!'"

"I hadn't thought of that," Ford confessed.

"Get Mage Reedis and have him confirm it," the prince ordered. "I'll have him brought to father to confirm."

"That should do, he saw it," Knox murmured to Ford.

"I don't expect you back until the morning," the prince said, waving them away with a look like he was conveying a great favor.

Ford and Knox bowed their way out of the room.

Captain Ford sensed trouble even before he pulled his horse to halt beside the *Spite*. The normal hustle of a ship's crew, even just a watch crew, was

absent.

"Ahoy the ship!" Knox yelled as he jumped down from his horse. He grunted as he shook out his legs and gave Ford a look that mirrored his own. Knox raised his voice and called again, "Ahoy the ship!"

Ford moved quickly toward the gantry, crossing the distance between wharf and ship in scant moments.

A shape appeared on the deck in the darkness. "Did someone call?"

Ford recognized the voice of Newman, the mechanic, his voice coming from the stern of the ship near his steam engine. The soot-covered man was a good head taller than Ford with thick black hair tied back and a red beard beginning to gray — all covered with bits of ash and soot, making him resemble some strange snow-covered half-giant.

"Indeed we did, Mr. Newman," Ford said. "But we didn't mean to disturb your labors. We were expecting one of our men to be on watch."

Newman snorted and shook his head. "They're all gone!"

"What?" Ford said, glancing around, hoping his eyes would prove the other a liar. "I said that there was to be a watch kept, that only some were to go on leave."

"Well, sir, it seems they didn't listen, did they?" Newman said with a sour look. "It's not just your men, my men scarpered as well."

"What?" Knox said. "You're the only one left? What about lieutenant Jens?"

"He was the first to leave," Newman said, spitting in derision. "Said there was no good staying on a cursed ship with no hope of pay."

"Pay?" Ford repeated angrily.

"I can't say I don't see their point," Newman said. "The prince promised a guinea and then welshed on it. They said if he couldn't pay a guinea, why should they believe that he could pay a pound?"

"So where are they?" Knox asked. "Let me find them —"

"Lieutenant Jens has shipped out on the *Warrior*," Newman said.

"What? When?" Knox asked. Captain Ford couldn't speak, he was so dismayed.

"He left first, took four seamen with him," Newman said. "Then the rest took off." He added bitterly, "And then my stokers when my back was turned."

"So there's no one left?" Knox said.

"Indeed."

"Where is the mage?" Ford asked.

Newman pointed up the road. "He went for a bite to eat, last I heard. He was gone when all this happened."

"Let's find him," Ford said, turning back toward the gantry.

"Should I stay here, sir?" Knox asked.

"Yes, wait for Marder," Ford replied.

"Reedis?" Ford said, sitting opposite the purple mage.

"Captain?"

"Are you almost done?" Ford said, eyeing the dishes overflowing the table. "The prince has asked me for your opinion on something of import."

Reedis motioned for him to continue while helping himself to another mouthful of meat.

"We found a body of a woman near where we found where the wyvern must have fallen," Ford said.

"But no wyvern?"

"No," Ford said. "But the woman was injured in a manner that seemed to match the wyvern's injuries."

"And you're wondering if the woman was the wyvern and somehow magically transformed?" Reedis guessed, stabbing another forkful of meat.

"Yes."

"I don't know much about wyverns. I know they look to Ophidian and I've heard that they're twin-

souled," Reedis said after a moment spent blissfully chewing and swallowing his morsel. Ford wondered how the man could be so thin and eat so much.

"Twin-souled?"

"Indeed," Reedis said after swallowing once more. "They burn so brightly that two souls are required to create them."

"How is that possible?"

Reedis shrugged, stabbing carrots and parsnips with his fork and shovelling them into this mouth.

"Could you tell if someone was magically transformed?" Ford asked, waiting for the other man to swallow.

"No," Reedis said. "But there might be some up in the King's court who could."

"The prince prefers not to ask them," Ford said with a sour look. Would the man never stop eating? Ford had been hungry when he'd entered the tavern but, now, his appetite was quite gone.

"They're a bunch of old women," Reedis said after swallowing his next mouthful, "doubtless

they'd spout off to everyone in the kingdom, the king included."

"Doubtless," Ford agreed, hiding his surprise in finding the mage in agreement with the prince. "But without a body, I've got a problem."

"You mean the prince has a problem," Reedis said, laying his fork down on his now empty plate.

"Which means that *I've* got a problem," Ford agreed with a sigh.

"So, where is this body?"

"In a grave not far from where the wyvern fell," Ford said. "It's too dark now to look for it."

"Indeed," Reedis said, rising from the table. Ford rose with him. "I'm staying here this evening."

"Shall I call for you in the morning?"

"You may," Reedis allowed. "But not too early, I'm quite fatigued from all the exertions of the day."

"The sooner the better," Ford said.

"I can't do magic without rest," Reedis said. He paused to think. Finally, he nodded to himself, saying, "Noon. I should be able then."

Chapter Six: A Wyvern's Corpse (89)

Ford bit back an angry retort and forced himself to say instead, "Very well, I'll see you then."

Chapter Seven: Captain of Nothing

aptain Ford spent the night aboard the *Spite*, alone. He woke shivering the next morning, wishing that the cooks hadn't deserted along with the rest of the crew. He made his way to the galley, started the fire and warmed himself a cup of tea. When he'd finished that, he went on deck.

A fog had engulfed the airship and for a moment Ford feared that perhaps the ship had lifted skywards in the night but then a gust blew the fog into tatters and he found himself looking at the buildings around him and the gantry amidships.

"Ahoy the ship!" a voice called from a patch still hidden in darkness. It was Knox.

"Come aboard!" Ford called back. The boatswain swarmed over the wooden gantry and knuckled his forehead in a salute to the captain. He glanced around the ship and spit sourly at the lack of

men.

"I was hoping some of the lads might have come back," Knox said.

"I'm afraid that their assessment was too accurate — if the prince would welsh on a guinea, what hope had they of their pay?"

"Well," Knox said with a shrug, "they'll never know now."

"True," Ford allowed. He gestured to the street. "I'm supposed to meet mage Reedis at noon and we'll go see the woman's body once more."

"To see if it's the wyvern?" Knox guessed.

"To see if his magic might tell us if it is," Ford said.

"Good enough," Knox said. He glanced around the ship and then added, "Will you need a hand?"

Ford shook his head. "I need you to stay here and guard the ship. See if you can get any of the lads to return."

"I'll try, captain," Knox said, his tone doubtful.

"That's all I can ask."

Captain Ford found Reedis at the same table, busily ingesting a half dozen eggs and countless slices of bacon. *Perhaps he has worms.*

"Ah, good morning, captain!" Reedis called, gesturing for the other to join him at the table. "I trust you had a restful sleep?"

"Well enough," Ford allowed. "And you?"

"The same," Reedis said, stuffing his mouth with a whole egg.

A maid came by and served Ford with a glass of water, delightfully chilled. Ford eyed it in surprise and Reedis pointed a finger at himself. "I did them a favor with some cold magic, and they let me stay here whenever I want."

"That's some magic," Ford agreed.

Reedis leaned forward and whispered conspiratorially, "It won't last, of course. So I'm eating as much as I can before the spell fades."

Ford raised an eyebrow in surprise. His face creased into a frown as a sudden thought occurred to him but Reedis answered his unspoken question with a dismissive wave of his hand, "It's not quite the same magic as the balloons, I assure you."

"Those spells won't wear off?"

"Oh, no! They'll wear off, sure enough," Reedis said with a bark of laughter. "But not while I'm still aboard!"

"So the *Spite* can't fly without you?"

"Surely you knew that already, Captain?" Ford said, chasing his egg with a handful of bacon.

"I did," Ford said. A moment later, he asked, "And does the King?"

"I worked mostly with Her Majesty and the prince," Reedis said. "The King would have nothing to do with me because he's sworn to Ametza."

"And you're not?"

"A mage that makes fire magic?" Reedis asked, his eyes dancing. He shook his head. "No, the goddess of water is not my patron."

"Nor is Ophidian, I imagine."

"Indeed," Reedis agreed. He made a face. "Ophidian's a fickle god, I wouldn't want to trust my life to such."

"So who do you serve that your magic provides hot and cold?" Ford asked.

Reedis placed a finger alongside his nose to show that Ford was being too nosy to ask.

"No offense," Ford said quickly. He needed this man.

"None taken," Reedis said. "But the less you know of magic, the better."

"Hmm," Ford considered that. "Actually, I think I should like to know enough that I wouldn't have to rely on you."

Reedis' eyes widened at that admission and Ford continued quickly, "Not that I don't appreciate your efforts and company but just in case something rendered you incapacitated and I needed to power the ship by myself."

"Captain," Reedis began in a gentle tone, "you

not only have to know my magic but also how that fireman Newman manages his flames."

"Are you saying he's a mage, too?"

"No," Reedis said sourly. "Of course not. But he's worked with them — and me, even — in the past to get his infernal engine to behave the way it does." Reedis paused, nabbed another slice of bacon and chewed on it thoughtfully before continuing, "No, just as you were dependent upon sailmakers and shipwrights when you were captain of a seaship, you are dependent upon Newman for the steam engine and me for your lifting balloons." He gave Ford a genial nod. "If I might be so bold, I'd recommend that you stick to doing what you know rather than trying to master such arcane arts."

"I see," Ford said. After a moment, he said, "But when on the sea I had the chance to throw myself on its mercies if the ship or the sails failed me. I don't have the same choice up in the air."

Reedis nodded and gave the captain an attentive look.

"If the dragon had flamed our balloons, there would have been nothing you could do to save us," Ford guessed. Reedis winced at the notion then, reluctantly, nodded. "I was wondering, however, if there might be a way to build a special spell that could be used quickly. A spell that would inflate a spare balloon or two so that men could escape on them earthwards to safety, just as we do with a life jacket."

"A life sphere?" Reedis joked, cocking his head at the notion. A moment later, he nodded. "You know, I *do* believe it could be done!"

"I was thinking of it last night, thinking of how we could have saved poor Havenam," Ford admitted.

"How was his widow?" Reedis asked somberly.

"She was furious," Ford said. "She threw things at me, cursed me."

"She did?" Reedis was surprised.

Ford nodded. "You see," he said, "I'd convinced Havenam to join my crew by convincing *her* that it would be safer up in the air than on the sea."

"Oh," the other said sympathetically.

"And now the crew's deserted," Ford continued, encouraged by the understanding of the other. "They said that if the prince could welsh on a bet, he'd welsh on their wages, too."

"Quite probably," Reedis agreed.

"Does that not worry you, too?"

"The prince and his mother were the only ones who considered the advantages of an airship," Reedis said. "It was through their patronage that I am where I find myself this day."

"Riding out to view the corpse of a woman in hopes that she's the wyvern?" Ford asked in bitter humor.

Reedis snorted in amusement. "Well, not quite *that*, perhaps, but certainly the first of my breed."

"Your breed?"

"I'll make a fortune when it comes time to take apprentices," Reedis said with a smug look.

Ford leaned back in his chair, startled by the novel concept. "I suppose you will, at that."

"But," Reedis said, raising a hand in caution, "before I can do that, I must first prove the efficacy of our airship against flying creatures."

"Like this wyvern?"

"Indeed," Reedis agreed, laying his fork on his plate and pushing back from the table. "So, Captain, shall we go see this body?"

Ford rose with him, a smile on his face.

"Mr. Reedis," he said, extending his hand, "I believe this is the beginning of a beautiful relationship."

"Indeed," Reedis said, taking his hand and shaking it firmly. "I had thought we were probably in the same boat." Ford snorted in amusement. Reedis' smile broadened. "As it were."

Mage Reedis needed no instruction in horsemanship even if he had a bad seat and tended to saw on his mount's reins. He and Ford made good

time. Captain Ford had obtained a shovel, assuring the mage that he knew where they could get a wagon if the need presented itself.

They rode in companionable silence, sweating with the sun beating down upon them.

"If you get too hot, let me know," Reedis said as he adjusted his hat against the sun's glare.

"Why? Do you have a spare hat?" Ford asked, regretting that he hadn't brought his with him.

Reedis smiled. "Better, I'm a mage of hot and cold." He waved his hands and suddenly Ford found himself cooled by a small but steady cold breeze.

"I can't see how you couldn't make your fortune with just *that* magic," Ford said as the sweat evaporated from his head.

"It's moment magic," Reedis said. Seeing the other's confusion he explained, "I can only make it in the moment, I can't prepare the spell ahead of time."

"Whoever could do that would be rich, then," Ford said.

"It was partly as a result of this simple magic

that I convinced the queen to fund our airship," Reedis said.

"A hot day and you provided the wind?" Ford guessed.

"Indeed," Reedis agreed with a smile. "That and the wind covered the sounds of a rather indecorous liaison the queen was having."

"Ah!" Ford said. He gestured to the left at the fork in the road and they moved down it. A moment later he pulled up and pointed to the field of wyvern's flowers. The field was full of the blue, pungent flowers.

"I see," Reedis said, scanning the field and finding the scar of a fallen beast. "They say that wyverns seek these flowers when they're about to die."

"Really?" Ford said in surprise. "I hadn't heard that."

"So you've learned something this day," Reedis said with a smile. "Let us go to this gravesite and see what else we can learn."

"Indeed," Ford said, taking the mage's favorite word for his own.

Chapter Eight: A Grave Revisited

Reedis pled the fragility of his bones when it came time to exhume the grave for the second time in as many days, leaving Captain Ford to strain with the shovel, cooled by Reedis' occasional magics.

When the body was revealed, Reedis peered down and examined it with a hand to his face.

"She was no beauty, that I'll say," the mage said as he took in the woman's face.

"I think she looked better yesterday," Ford said, finding his hand rising to protect his nose as well. The decay was beginning to take stronger hold. "I think this night in the dirt has altered her features." He glanced up from the dirt to the mage. "Can you tell if she was the wyvern?"

"No, she wasn't," Reedis said. "She'd only be

half of the wyvern at best."

"So why is she a woman and not a beast?"

"I think that this was the human half of the beast," Reedis said with a frown. He raised his hands and moved them in a widening circle, muttering a spell under his breath. A moment later the spell burst over the corpse and the two jumped back as they saw a larger, shadowy creature in the grave. It had white and gold scales. It was the wyvern they'd shot from the skies. "Yes," Reedis said in a fainter voice, "this is the human half of our twin-souled wyvern."

The image faded and Ford rocked back on his heels. He glanced at the woman once more and then leaped out of the grave.

"So where is the *other* half?" Ford said when he was at the same level as the mage.

Mage Reedis shook his head. "I can't possibly say."

"Sire, it's true, I saw it myself," Reedis said to the prince as Captain Ford recounted their adventure in the fields two hours past.

"So you are saying that I killed only *half* of the wyvern!" the prince roared. "Captain Ford, can you imagine me asking my father for *half* of a triumph?"

"Sire," Ford began slowly, "Mage Reedis is of the opinion that perhaps the other half of the wyvern is still alive and looking for a human host."

"A host?" the prince repeated, the fire of anger dimming in his eyes. He turned to Reedis. "And if so, what then?"

"They'd form a new wyvern, sire," the mage said in a small voice.

"I can *not* allow that to happen!" the prince said. He turned to Ford. "You cannot allow that to happen, captain."

Ford groped for something to say in reply.

"At the moment, sire," Reedis spoke up hesitantly. The prince turned a stony gaze to him and Reedis swallowed nervously before continuing, "At the moment, I — and Captain Ford — are willing to swear that the wyvern was hit —"

Chapter Eight: A Grave Revisited 105

"By me," the prince interjected.

"Sire?" Reedis asked.

"The wyvern was hit by me," the prince said. "It was my excellent gunnery that hit the beast while the other shots flew wide."

"Um, yes," Reedis said. "Although honesty compels me to admit that my attention was directed in keeping our airship flying, sire."

"If I wanted honesty, mage, I would ask for it," the prince told him with a gleam in his eyes. He chuckled, apparently amused at his own words. A moment later, more seriously, he said, "What I need, *Captain*, is for you, the mage here and all your crew to stand in the presence of my royal father and declare the truth to him and his court."

"Ah, sire," Ford began slowly. The prince's gaze hardened angrily. "I'm afraid that the crew are not available —"

"What?" the prince howled.

"I let them take leave, sire," Ford temporized, "and I'm afraid they're in no condition to swear before the King." *Condition, location — all much the same, isn't it?* Ford thought to

himself.

The prince glared at the two men then nodded. "Very well, I'll explain that they are busy getting ready for our next conquest."

Reedis glanced nervously toward Ford.

"Next conquest, sire?" Ford asked.

"Well, we certainly can't tell my father that we're going after the *same* wyvern, can we?" the prince said. He clenched a fist and raised it between them. "If I am to swear that the beast is dead, I'd best make certain, shouldn't I?" He lowered his fist and in a more moderate tone, almost to himself, continued, "And that way I'll be able to claim *two* of the beasts."

"I see," Reedis said in the awkward silence that descended after that pronouncement. "You know, sire, there's a chance that the wyvern half of this twin-soul has found another human here in our fair kingdom."

"Perhaps even in this town," Ford said in quick agreement.

"Then why have we not seen it?" the prince demanded.

"The form left in the grave was that of a woman," Reedis said. "So I must imagine that the wyvern half is looking for — maybe even now has found — a suitable partner." The prince gave him a confused a look. "A woman."

"A woman?" the prince repeated. Reedis nodded. The prince frowned. He drew a deep breath. "Very well, prepare yourselves for the royal presence and then, after, you shall go hunting this beast."

"Well, *that's* over," Ford said as he and Reedis found themselves back outside of the palace, waiting with the crowds at the triumph balcony, watching the prince waving and smiling broadly and waving the glowing blue amulet of Ametza that hung from his neck to the crowd below. Every second wave or so, he'd raise a large red velvet bag that was overflowing with gold and gems — his added reward.

"It would have been nice if he'd given us more

than a thank you," Reedis said, gesturing to the royal purse in view above them.

"What, *Sir* Reedis, do you not revel in your royal appointment?" Ford said mockingly.

"I do not see you doing the same, Sir Ford," Reedis replied with a touch of frost in his voice.

Ford sighed and shrugged. "The honor doesn't put food on the table or crew on my ship."

"Didn't the prince give you full rein to raid the royal goal?" Reedis reminded him.

Ford snorted. "Indeed, and how well will you, Sir Reedis, sleep at night with my crew of cutthroats and thieves guarding your rest?"

Reedis replied with a sour look and started to speak but before he could someone in the crowd shouted: *"Fire!!"*

And the crowd scattered in fear and confusion. Ford kept a hold of Reedis despite the buffeting and dragged the mage back to the tavern where they sought rest and refuge.

"You!" the tavern-keeper shouted when he

caught sight of the mage. "What did you *do?*"

"Me?" Reedis cried in surprise. "What are you talking about?"

"My food! It's all *ashes!*" the tavern-keeper said. "That cooler of yours turned into a fireball not twenty minutes ago!"

"I had nothing to do with that, I can assure you!" Reedis cried in surprise. "I was with the King, receiving a knighthood."

"Well you can take your knighthood elsewhere, sir knave, your company is not welcome here," a woman's voice — the tavern keeper's wife — shrieked. "Be gone before I find a mage of curses and spite you!"

Ford pulled Reedis out of the tavern and they stood on the cobbled street, wondering what to do next.

Finally Ford said, "There's food on the *Spite*, not great fare, but something."

"And your cook?"

Ford gave him a sour smile. "Perhaps Knox can

cook for us."

Reedis shrugged and gestured to Ford. "Lead on, Sir Ford, and we shall have our repast on your royal airship."

"Indeed, Sir Reedis," Ford said, "My ship shall be proud to have the royal ballooneer grace its timbers with his presence."

The two laughed, locked arms and strolled back toward the ship and the gantry.

Knox was still there but eager to leave them as, "I've got to get home to the missus. There was a disturbance and a fire and she's right worried."

"Go!" Ford said, waving his last crewman off. "We'll talk in the morning."

Knox seemed reluctant to leave but knuckled his forehead in a salute and trotted quickly off the ship and down the street.

"Do you think you'll see him in the morning?" Reedis wondered.

"Aye," Ford said. "But whether he'll stay when he learns about our new crew..." his voice trailed

off. He shook himself and jerked his head toward the hatchway. "I've a bottle in my quarters, and Knox swore he kept the galley fire going."

"If he didn't," Reedis said, "I know someone who can magic a fire to life."

The galley fire was dead in the morning and Reedis could do nothing to revive because they were out of wood to burn.

They drank brackish water and regretted that they'd finished not just one but *two* bottles of wine between them. They were just motivated enough to search for some place that might feed them when a royal messenger clambered — loudly! — up the gantry and shouted for them.

"Sir Reedis! Sir Ford! His Royal Highness requires your presence!" the page bellowed in proper form.

"Ahhh!" Reedis said, raising his hands to his ears. "Can he not do it more quietly?"

"I'll bet you wish you were a mage of sound, right about now," Ford added grimly. He waved to the page and asked in a quiet voice, "And does his royal highness have transport for us?"

"I have two horses with me," the page said.

"Wonderful!" Reedis groaned. "Hooves on cobblestones! What a charming sound so early in the morning!"

"It is not early, sir," the page replied stiffly. He glanced upwards to the sky. "The sun is nearing noon, if you'd see."

"Ahh, I'd prefer not, if it's all well enough with you," Reedis replied. Ford jerked his head toward the gantry, regretted the motion, and gestured with one hand for the page to lead them away.

"She's here!" the prince bellowed, stomping down the hallway toward them as soon as they alighted their horses. "The shaman at the temple said

that she'd seen her!"

"What?" Reedis asked in puzzlement while wincing in pain from the prince's voice. "Who?"

"The girl?" Ford, whose seaman's life gave him a better tolerance for wine on an empty stomach, guessed.

"Yes, indeed!" the prince said. "She wouldn't give us the name, saying some rubbish about oaths to Ametza —" the prince caught himself and glanced nervously toward the port and the sea beyond, hoping not to gain an inundation in response for his inopportune words — "but she *saw* the girl. She was about to be married, can you imagine?."

"Imagine her husband on their wedding night," Reedis muttered to Ford. The comment caused the other to splutter in amusement.

"What?" the prince said. "Do you doubt me?"

"No, sire," Ford said quickly. "I was just wondering — where is your amulet?"

The prince's face clouded in pure loathing. "Stolen! It and my jewels were stolen!" He frowned

in memory. "We couldn't catch the thief, he got away when some idiot shouted 'fire!' at the ceremony."

"We were there!" Reedis exclaimed.

"Well, why didn't you catch him?"

"We didn't see him, sire, we were overwhelmed by the crowd," Ford explained.

"So were my guards," the prince grumbled.

The two newly knighted royals exchanged looks: they both wondered how hard the guard looked and whether the soldiers were as well-rewarded as Ford's sailors.

"What do you desire of us, my prince?" Ford said, going down on one knee.

The prince wiggled his fingers in indication that Ford should stand. "Do?" the prince said. "Why find her, of course! Kill her and show her the King's justice!"

"Don't you mean show her the King's justice and then kill her?" Reedis asked.

"I meant what I said!" the prince roared, waving them away. "And don't come back until she's dead!"

"ell, *that* was a help," Reedis muttered when they were safely back on the street. "What do we do now?"

"Can you use magic to track her?" Ford asked.

The mage shook his head. "I'm a wizard of hot —"

"— and cold magic," Ford finished in unison with him, shaking his head bitterly. "So we'll have to see what we can do on our own." He started walking.

"Where are we going?"

"Back to the ship," Ford said. "At least we'll get a cup of tea."

"We'll have to get more water first," Reedis warned.

Ford shrugged agreement and picked up his pace, noting sourly that the prince hadn't seen to offer them horses for the ride back. "Perhaps Knox

will have an idea."

Knox, did indeed have an idea. He helped them get water and make tea and the three sat at the small table in Ford's captain's quarters.

"That apprentice, didn't he seem shifty?"

"He did," Ford agreed, worried that he would find himself making another trip out of town. "Why do you ask?"

"Well, he mentioned the mechanical, Ibb, didn't he?"

Ford nodded.

"So, you know this Ibb, don't you sir?"

"Are you suggesting we talk with him?" Ford guessed. He grimaced as he mulled the notion over then knocked back his cup in one gulp and rose. "Come along then, let's see what Ibb knows."

"He's a mechanical?" Reedis asked, rising himself and looking worried.

"He is," Ford said. "Many people don't associate with him because he worships a different god. They say the mechanicals were an ancient people who

decided that they could cheat the Ferryman by transferring their souls into the cold cogs and gears of machines rather than frail flesh."

"What's he look like?" Reedis asked.

"His soul is in a tall, stocky metal body topped with a metal head that seems a mixture of gold and brass, with cogs, and two glowing red gems for eyes. He's got metal eyebrows, too." Ford shrugged. "His voice is deep, like it comes from a cave, but after a while you don't notice."

"How long have you known him?"

"I knew him from years ago when he first came here," Ford said. "In fact, we rescued him when my ship, the *Sprite*, took the corsair that had captured him. He helped us by giving us a list of improvements for our rigging — we got three knots more speed after that."

"Ah!" Reedis said, encouraged. "So he's in your debt."

"I'd count him more a friend than a debtor," Ford said as they made their way back onto the street.

Ford set a good clip.

"Mechanical men have peculiar loyalties," Reedis said cautiously.

Ford raised an eyebrow. "Swindled one, did you?"

"Sir Ford! I must protest your language!"

"Well, how else do you describe that fire box that so infuriated your late benefactor?"

"Fire box?" Knox asked, glancing between the two. "And why does he call you Sir Ford, sir?"

"The King seems to have a particularly dark sense of humor," Ford explained. He pointed to Reedis. "He knighted us last night."

"Knighted!" Knox exclaimed. A moment later, he said shrewdly, "And did he pay you by any chance, captain?"

"As I said," Ford replied, shaking his head, "he has a dark sense of humor."

"So the lads were right," Knox said to himself.

"I don't know about that, boatswain," Ford said. "We're not due our wages 'til the end of the

month and that's a fortnight yet."

"There's much that can happen in a fortnight," the boatswain muttered darkly.

"Bad *and* good," Ford reminded him. They entered a broad street and he picked up the pace.

Minutes later they turned down a side street and came to a well-appointed but old building. Ford strode forward and wrapped on the door, calling loudly, "Open up, you clanker! We got questions for you!"

"Just a moment!" a mechanical voice called back. Ford glanced at the others and crossed his arms, waiting. Some moments later, the door opened and the mechanical man gestured them inside.

Knox came in slowly but Ford rushed in, going from one thing to the next, rushing about the room in excitement. Reedis, inspired by the captain was no less inquisitive.

"What have you been doing lately?" Ford asked, slapping a hand — carefully — on the metal man's shoulder. He'd sprained his wrist years back

so he knew that the metal was hard and unyielding.

"Many things," Ibb replied. "I heard you are flying an airship these days." The mechanical man clanked as he shook his head. "I think you were safer on the sea."

"Aye, safer!" Ford agreed heartily. "We lost Havenam. You remember him, my young midshipman from all those years back?"

"Is he still young?" Ibb asked. "And a — a midship-man?"

"He's dead," Ford said sourly. "A dragon toppled him from the tops of the balloons and he fell to his death."

"That is sad?" Ibb said in a voice devoid of emotion. Ford knew that the mechanical had trouble with the feelings of others, having not had any for hundreds of years or more.

"It is," Ford said. "His widow cursed me when I brought his body home."

"Was it a good curse?"

"The words were powerful," Reedis spoke up

for the first time, "but she hasn't a drop of magic in her."

Ibb rotated to look at Reedis. "And you are?"

"I'm sorry, where are my manners?" Ford apologized. Before he could continue, Ibb said, "I do not know. Have you misplaced them?"

"Probably," Knox muttered, his eyes dancing with amusement. To Ford he said, "I'd forgotten what a corker Mr. Ibb is!"

"This is mage Reedis," Ford said, ignoring the boatswain. "He is responsible for the hot and cold magic that raises the airship."

"And Mr. Newman is responsible for the air propellers that move it," Ibb said, nodding gravely. A moment later, he asked, "And where is Mr. Newman?"

"Cursing his luck," Knox said in a low voice.

Ford ignored him. "He is well and with the ship, my *Spite*."

"I thought your ship was named *Sprite*," Ibb said.

"It was, until the King took it into service," Ford said. "Then she was renamed."

"A good practice," Ibb said. "Although there are air sprites, I'm given to understand that this ship is to be the spite of flying fire beings."

"Indeed," Ford said. "Which leads me to our journey here."

"How so?"

"We shot a wyvern," Ford explained. "The dragon we were shooting at got away, after killing poor Havenam."

"Only we didn't find a wyvern's body when we went looking," Knox spoke up. "We found a woman's body."

"Did you find her in a field of wyvern flowers?" Ibb asked.

"Why?" Ford said, his brows narrowing. "Do you know something of this?"

"I know that wyverns like to die in wyvern flowers," Ibb said. "And that they're twin-souled, part human, part soul of fire." He turned slowly, first

toward the back door and then around to them. "I could inquire of more."

"What can we tell you?"

Ibb clanked backwards a step, then moved to the right, reaching for something by the door. Ford followed him with his eyes and saw a coat rack with an umbrella sticking up. The mechanical reached for it.

"I would not inquire of you," Ibb said, moving toward the door. "I would inquire of those more knowledgeable, naturally."

His progress was interrupted by another loud knocking on his door. "Open up! In the King's name!"

Ibb turned to Ford. "What is this?"

"There was a theft, the prince's amulet and jewels were stolen," Ford said. "They're looking for it."

"Indeed!" Ibb said. "They will doubtless impede my journey." He gestured toward the back door. "Perhaps you will not want to handle this delay. If you go that way, please open the barrel just

by the door."

"What's in it?" Knox asked.

"Something to persuade guests not to linger," the mechanical replied. Ibb started rumbling in the rusty noise that was his version of a laugh.

Ford smiled at him and nodded. "We'll be on our way then."

"Safe journey!"

"And more knowledge," Ford said, completing the farewell of the mechanicals. The three moved to the back and, at Ford's gesture, Knox lifted the lid on the small bucket by the door. Instantly, he turned a horrible shade of green and rushed past them out the door.

"What was that?" Ford asked as he joined Knox and Reedis safely away from the horrid smell.

"I don't know," Knox said. "Smelled like someone vomited something horrible." He

shuddered. "I think I saw a bit of eel, too."

Through the back door they heard someone bellow: "What is that, it smells awful!"

"Something I've been working on," Ibb's mechanical voice replied. "Gentlemen, let us move this conversation outside, or soon the fumes will become toxic for your lungs."

Ford smiled and gestured to the others. "Come on, let's go!"

"Where to, sir?" Knox asked.

"We're going to the goal, of course," Ford said.

"Whatever for?"

"To pick up more crew, no doubt," Reedis muttered darkly.

Ford raised a hand. "I'm hoping it won't come to that."

Catching the look of relief on Knox's face, he added in vile humor, "Perhaps we'll just get some stokers for Mr. Newman." He was rewarded with a look of ill-repressed horror from the boatswain.

"If not crew, then what, Sir Ford?" Reedis asked.

"Answers," Ford replied. He picked up his pace forcing the others to follow in silence.

The jail was in turmoil with guards clattering about, seeming in great spirits.

"What is it?" Ford asked as they approached.

"For a penny, I'll tell you," a small child said, approaching with a hand held out.

"For less, my mage will freeze you to death," Ford growled. He'd been dealing with urchins all his life, having started out as one himself.

The small child's eyes widened in horror as she took in Ford's expression, saw the purple robes of the mage and the rough features of the boatswain.

"They — they caught the thief," the child said, pointing toward the jail. "Caught him in the inn, of all places! The madame turned him in!"

Ford frowned, reached into his pocket but, before he could pull a penny as a reward, the child scampered off as quick as her thin legs could take her.

"What now?" Reedis asked. "They've caught

the prince's thief."

"We still have to find the girl," Ford said darkly. He headed to the jail. "We should talk with the thief."

"And scout for crew," Reedis muttered.

"Possibly," Ford said. He asked the mage, "How soon could you lift the ship again?"

"I'm ready enough now," Reedis said. "Although there's one thing I'd like to do, first." Ford gave him an inquiring look. Reedis glanced briefly to the boatswain before replying, "That little project you mentioned."

"Oh! Oh, yes!" Ford said. "It might be useful." He gestured to jail. "This first, I think."

The King's Jail was a musty stone building set at the worst part of the dockyards. Ford had known it of old and avoided it as much as he could.

"What do you want?" the guard at the gate asked them in surly tones.

"Respect, for a King's knight, for one," Reedis replied, drawing himself up to his full height.

"For two," Ford said, his lips twitching as he

pointed to himself.

"Captain Ford?" the guard said, brows narrowing.

"It's Captain Sir Ford these days," Ford corrected airily.

"I'd heard you'd gone and blown away in a gale," the guard said.

"I blew back again, Sykes," Ford said, his tone becoming harder. "You've prisoners and I've a writ from the prince to inspect them."

"A writ?" the guard repeated. He glanced at Reedis and Knox, whom he recognized with a nod. Knox responded with a growl of intense dislike. "Well, I suppose that's all right then," Sykes said. "I'll need a shilling from each of you."

"You'll need to hope the mage doesn't get in a temper and boil your skin off your worthless bones," Ford snapped, moving past the guard as though he didn't exist.

Sykes took a step backwards frightened, eyeing the mage warily. "H-he could do that?" he asked

Knox.

"Worse," Knox replied striding past.

The three stopped a pace later, their hands going to their noses.

"You get used to the stench!" Sykes called to their backs in grim humor. "We don't call them the scum of the earth without reason, you know!"

"Come on," Ford said, regretting the breath the words required of him. Having breathed, and finding that he could still breathe, regardless of the foul odors which assailed him — worse than Ibb's bucket of vomit — he called to Sykes, "Where's the thief?"

"Second on the left!" Sykes called back. "We keep the ones the King wants to hang close by the door."

A shape darted to the bars as they approached and Ford thought the look on the thief's face was eager, expectant almost, until he saw them.

"Who are you?" the thief growled. "What do you want?"

"Manners, at least," Knox rasped back, drawing his dirk and banging it, flat-bladed against the thief's fingers wrapped around the bars. The thief was too quick and jerked back with snake-like speed, leaving Knox's weapon to clatter loudly against the metal.

The thief smiled at Knox's discomfort. "You have to have manners, first, dog." He glanced toward Ford without recognition but his eyes flared as he took in Reedis' purple robes and he slammed against the bars once more. "You! Murderer!"

"What?" Reedis said, stepping back in surprise.

"You burn and you freeze," the thief said. He laughed bitterly. "I saw what you did at the tavern. You can be sure I put a fix to *that*."

"What?" Reedis said again.

"What are you?" Ford said, his eyes narrowing as he examined the thief carefully, as though looking for something else.

"Nothing your ears will hear," the thief snarled lowly. He cocked his head at Ford, considering. "Are you the captain, then?"

"Captain Sir Ford commands the king's airship, and you'd best not forget that," Knox said supportively.

"Ah! So it was you who killed her," the thief said.

"What's your name?" Ford asked conversationally. "I'd like us to at least speak civilly."

"My name is Jarin and I've no need to speak to you," the thief spat. "I don't talk to carrion or the dead."

"The woman in the wyvern field? You knew her?" Ford guessed, startled by the thief's reference to the dead.

Jarin jerked back as if struck. He was silent for longer than usual before replying, "I don't know what you're talking about."

"We're looking for a girl," Reedis said. "Have you seen her?"

"I've seen many a girl," Jarin replied with a leer. "You'd have to be more specific."

"What do you know of wyverns?" Ford said.

"Why did you steal the prince's amulet?"

"Ametza's bauble?" Jarin replied with a snort. "It means nothing to her, you know. Nor me."

"So it was the jewels," Ford guessed. "You stole them."

"They were owed me and mine," Jarin said. "I stole nothing."

"The King thinks differently," Knox muttered.

"The King thinks that *boy* is his son," Jarin snorted. "He is ignorant, lazy, indolent, and soon to lose all that he values."

"You'll lose your life before that," Ford said, although noting that no one would gainsay his words.

"I shall dance on your grave," Jarin said, eyes glinting. "I am just waiting —" he cut himself off and shook his head. "I'm tired, I shall rest now." He turned away from them and went to one of the dark corners of his cell.

"Come on," Ford said, "we'll get no more from him." He motioned them to move on. "We need to

inspect the others that are here."

"For crew?" Knox asked in astonishment.

"At least we know where they *are*," Ford said mildly, moving toward the back of the jail.

They spent another twenty minutes in the jail. Ford identified four men he'd known of old — they were good workers when sober — and found another eight who might do in a pinch. That left him short four regular crew and four stokers. The thought of continuing the search in that horrid stench was too much for him and he jerked his head back to the entrance in a wordless order. Neither Reedis nor Knox objected.

Chapter Ten: Talent of Mine

Outside, Reedis said, "So what now?"

"Now, we find ourselves a warm meal and wait," Ford said, nodding toward the jail.

"What?" Knox said.

"We wait," Ford said. "And we keep a careful eye on the jail."

"They won't take our prisoners, sir," Knox said, "they've got nowhere to take them."

"Our thief made a mistake," Ford said. Knox and Reedis looked confused. "He said that he was waiting." He shrugged. "So we wait."

"What for, sir?"

"For whatever he is waiting for," Ford replied. Reedis gave him a dubious look. "The King will have his head this evening but our thief does not seem fearful. Clearly he expects something to aid him

before that time."

"There's an inn just down the road," Knox offered. "The food's not great but it's warm."

Ford gestured for him to lead. "By all means, boatswain, let us feast!"

The inn proved lively. It was run by a woman who was referred to as "the madame." The food was good but Ford suspected he'd be happier sleeping aboard his ship — and would be less likely to wake up with lice or worse.

"There's a huge crowd here tonight," Knox said, "more than usual."

"Why don't you see what is happening?" Ford suggested. Knox smiled and rose, heading off to a table at the far side of the bar. Ford followed him with his eyes and then stopped — rising precipitously from his chair.

"What?" Reedis asked from over his large, full plate, a fork poised just before his mouth.

"Stay there," Ford said, "I just want to check on something." He had spied a small child enter

the room, an urchin. She looked like the one who'd begged for a penny.

She spotted him as he approached and tried to sidle away but he called out, reaching into his pocket, "I just wanted to pay you."

"Sir?" the little girl said, glancing about for safety.

Ford showed her the copper penny. He pulled another from his pocket and showed it to her, too. "This other one is if you do something for me."

The girl sidled away, suddenly more wary than before. "What?"

"I need you to go back to the jail and keep an eye on that thief," Ford said.

"For that I'll take a shilling," the girl said boldly.

"Tuppence, no more," Ford countered. She thought about it, nodded, and put her hand out. Ford's eyebrows rose in astonishment. "I'll pay you when you've got news, not before!"

"So pay me," the girl said, with a hungry grin, "'cuz I've got news!"

"Sir, did you hear?" Knox came rushing over at that moment. "The thief's escaped!"

The girl's face fell.

"That was your news?" Ford guessed. He passed her the two pennies. She took them but gave him a look of confusion. "The first is from before. The second is half of what you would have got if you'd done the job."

The girl's face twisted as she considered this, then she nodded and clasped the pennies, turning in the same moment and vanishing into the crowd.

Ford turned to Knox. "How did he escape?"

"The door was wide open," Knox said, shrugging. "There are those who suspect magic."

"What about a simple pick?" Ford asked. Knox allowed that possibility with a shrug of his own.

"They say there was a girl who visited not much before and they ran off together," the urchin, who Ford had believed long gone, offered up shyly. "There's a reward, the prince says that they killed a woman in a wyvern field."

Ford sighed, reached into his pocket and pulled out two more pennies. "Do you know where they went, by any chance?"

"Pay me first," the girl demanded. With a heavy sigh, Ford put the pennies in her hand. She made them disappear into her thin shift, smiled at him and shook her head. Ford smiled again and she laughed, a light, airy laugh that seemed totally at odds with her situation. When she finished, Ford gave her a dark look but she just laughed again, saying, "Where does anyone go to escape?"

"Oh!" Ford said in sudden understanding. The others looked at him in surprise. "Come on, Knox, we're going to the docks!"

"My feet are killing me, is it much further?" Reedis complained as they spied the masts of ships dimly visible in the fading light. He glanced upwards. "What's that?"

"Snow," Ford said, following his gaze and catching sight of the first flakes. "An early fall but not unexpected."

"I'm going to freeze!" Reedis whined.

"Use one of your warming spells, then," Ford said with little sympathy.

"You cannot imagine how *difficult* it would be to warm anything in this cold," Reedis responded.

"Shh," Ford hissed. "Listen!"

"Krea!" a voice shouted in the distance toward two people not two hundred paces from them.

"That's the apprentice!" Knox said to Ford in surprise. His brow furrowed, "But who's Krea?"

"Shh!" Ford said again. Knox was right, it was Angus, the surly young apprentice they had met at the farm. Softly, he added, "If we are quiet, we may well find out." Ford gestured toward an overturned rowboat nearby and indicated that they should take shelter there.

A clanking in the distance, near the shout of the apprentice, alerted them to the presence of a

mechanical man.   Ford needed only one glance over his shoulder to determine that the mechanical was Ibb himself. Reedis saw him too and started to exclaim in surprise but Ford put a hand over his mouth warningly.

They reached the rowboat and their shadows blended with it. They listened. The light breeze brought some words toward them.

"How did you find me?" the girl, Krea, asked.

"It's a talent of mine," Ibb replied, trying to keep his booming voice quiet. Ford saw him wave in the direction of the apprentice. "I brought him. He needs to know what is happening."

The breeze took the next several exchanges away from them except for a few snippets.

"Is that why you're dressed as a boy?" the apprentice asked. Ford realized that the girl was dressed in pants.

Reedis tugged on Ford's sleeve and Ford turned to give him an irritated look only to find that the mage was pointing into the distance. There were

torches moving towards them. Many torches.

The mob had found the thief.

"Go!" Ibb bellowed, his voice carrying clearly in the night. Lower, he added, "I'll find you!"

Three darks shapes sprinted away, leaving the looming bulk of the mechanical to stand before the mob.

"Come on!" Ford called, urging the others to their feet. He started toward the mechanical man.

"Shouldn't we go after *them?*" Reedis asked, pointing at the fugitives.

"He said he'll find them, didn't he?" Ford said, not hiding his exasperation. Understanding dawned on the faces of the other two. "He can't do that if the mob tears him apart!"

He rushed to Ibb's side and raised his arms above his head, calling to the approaching torches, "Stop! In the King's name, stop! Your quarry is that way!" He pointed after the fleeing thief and the girl. The mob paused and seemed about to disregard him but he caught sight of a mounted guard. "You there!

I need your horse!"

"Two of them!" Reedis shouted, pointing toward another mounted guard. "Hand them over now, in the King's name!"

"And who are you to be using the King's — oh! It's you!" Sykes, the guard, said in a resigned tone.

"Us, indeed!" Ford cried. "Now get off your horses! Guard this mechanical and hold him — he knows something and I mean to learn it."

Reluctantly the two guards relinquished their mounts. Ford and Reedis climbed up in their stead. Ford looked down to Knox, saying, "Look after Mr. Ibb, if you would. We'll find you when we can."

"Aye, sir," Knox replied. "I'll be sure that nothing untoward occurs."

Ford sketched him a salute and urged his mount into a trot after the vanishing mob.

"However does he command so much loyalty?" Ibb rumbled in surprise to Knox.

"He doesn't," Knox replied. "His whole crew's deserted."

"Hmm," Ibb rumbled in response.

They were too late. Ford pulled up his reins as he heard a shrill screech and looked upwards to see a brilliant white wyvern — much younger than the one which had fallen to *Spite's* broadside — rise high into the air, crying in triumph and disappearing northwards into the night.

"Come on!" Ford called, urging his horse into a gallop and turning it back to the town.

"Where are we going?" Reedis cried in surprise, turning to follow him.

"To the jail!" Ford called back. "We're going to need a crew!"

"What?"

"We've got to follow that wyvern or the prince will have our heads!"

With a groan of pained agreement, the purple mage followed.

Far ahead, the winter wyvern flew on into the growing snowstorm.

All too quickly she was lost from sight.

Ready for more?

The next book in the Twin Souls series is *Frozen Sky*.
Click on the QR Code to get it now!

Acknowledgements

o book gets done without a lot of outside help.

We are so grateful to Jeff Winner for his marvelous cover art work.

We'd like to thank all our first readers for their support, encouragement, and valuable feedback.

Any mistakes or omissions are, of course, all our own.

About the Authors

 ward-winning authors The Winner Twins, Brit and Brianna, have been writing for over ten years, with their first novel (*The Strand*) published when they were twelve years old.

New York Times bestselling author Todd McCaffrey has written over a dozen books, including eight in the Dragonriders of Pern® universe.

Printed in Great Britain
by Amazon